A Dozen of Tamales

Slices of Life

Lena Zupcsek

A Dozen of Tamales
Copyright © 2024 by Lena Zupcsek

ISBN: 979-8894790770 (hc)
ISBN: 979-8894790756 (sc)
ISBN: 979-8894790763 (e)

The Reading Glass Books
1-888-420-3050
www.readingglassbooks.com
fulfillment@readingglassbooks.com

Table of Contents

To my Mami: You finally spread your angelic wings and roam between suns and moons. Hope you won't worry about me. I only have to live my life.

And to Teresa: I did it! Wish you will read and smile.

Chapter 1

I know where you come from!

"I made my hot chocolate from scratch," said Vasile, savoring the content of the colorful mug, holding it just right so its hundred percent custom-made, money back guarantee logo design was centered and equally away from his protective palms and could read "I'm a NURSE. What's your superpower?"

"You mean you scratched the top of your head, like Stan Laurel, and turned on the Keurig? That's your hot cocoa from scratch?" asked Onuțu getting out of the bathroom, with just a towel around his waist, poor copycat for Derek Morgan in Criminal Minds. He stepped on an unpopped popcorn kernel that was embedded into the kitchen carpet, recovered it from between his toes and threw it straight toward Vasile's head.

Somehow, his brother maneuvered the superpowered nurse's mug, just in time and at the right angle, to intercept and to alter the trajectory of the seed back into the carpet. "You missed me!" yelled Vasile, performing his favorite Duchenne smile, which Onuțu ignored completely. He disappeared into the pantry for a moment and when he returned, a box of cereal was balancing on his head. Pushing Vasile out of his way, he opened the kitchen cabinet and, carefully, picked a bowl from the shelf and poured a small mountain of cereal into it. Then he chose a tablespoon from one of the drawers and filled his mouth with the dry cereal.

"Mom's idea of healthy food will send us directly to the Emergency Room one of these days", he mumbled, then started reciting the nutrition facts: " six grams of fiber, iron eighteen milligrams, zinc, magnesium and phosphorus ten percent. Ten percent of what? The box? The bowl? No sugar added, great! Not a crumble of fat, thanks, Mom! Quinoa, flax, buckwheat.

What the heck is buckwheat? Hey, Siri!" The phone's screen lit suddenly, the colorful, cotton sugar-like floating sphere appeared and one of the most sexy voices of the twenty-first century was there, in the little kitchen, with the two boys: "Hm?". "What is amaranth?" asked Onuțu in a serious tone of voice. Siri poured out her finding: "Amaranth is a plant native to Mexico and Central America. It is a cosmopolitan genus of annual or short-lived perennial plants collectively known as amaranths. The leaves and seeds of this plant are edible and provide various nutritional benefits." Onuțu opened his mouth ready for his next question: "How do you know that?", but Siri cut in line: "This is from Medicinenet and Wikipedia". "Well, at least now I know that it is edible. If I want to know the benefits, I'll most probably read for the rest of the day about its chemical formula, what our ancestors used to do with it, how the grains travel from point A to point B on the Globe and, most importantly, what is going to do to me if I eat it. Which probably I won't because I'll be lost in knowledge and I'll forget that I was in the process of eating my breakfast! Why do we even have to go to college nowadays? All we need is Siri, Alexa or Google, a device and internet! And why can't we just have Cocoa puffs or Frosted flakes like we used to?! " He opened the refrigerator, grabbed the jug of almond milk and read the expiration date: April twenty-seven. What's today?" Gave a soft touch to the I-phone's screen with his index and eyed the date: Sunday, April 30. "Darn it! She always buys what's on sale and close to the expiration date! Now what should I do? I'm hungry!!!" In an effort to drench the flakes, he managed to spill milk on the counter, all around the bowl. He muttered: "The fiber in the super-duper cereal or the expired milk, or both, will give me the energy to run to the bathroom and sit on the throne for the rest of the day searching for "buckwheat". That's it! Here is the behind-the-scenes diabolical plan! This cereal will give me the runs and the body will have to use the stored resources. And I will lose weight! Ta-ta!" He wiped the mess with the sleeve of his hoodie, then sat down at the table starting a robotical adduction-abduction movement with his right hand, to and from the cereal bowl, while his attention span became solely dedicated to Gordon Ramsay's show running on the screen of his phone.

"Why did you even check the expiration date if you knew exactly you were going to drink it no matter what?" said Vasile letting the last drop of his hot cocoa trickle down his throat. And because Onuțu kept on pretending he was home alone, Vasile continued, like self-explaining : "We are out of cocoa k-cup pods, but I found this!" He reached the counter, snatched a 23 ounces plastic container of Hershey's, bestlife approved, natural unsweetened 100% cacao and butted in between Onuțu's face and Gordon Ramsay's fuming eyes. "Listen to this", he made himself heard, "it contains natural antioxidants found in tea and certain fruits and is part of a healthy diet and active lifestyle. In moderation, though." Vasile lowered his fizz for a second concluding more for himself: "That means I can't make it a habit? Still, imagine myself at seventy-five, in an interview conducted by Oprah's great-granddaughter, stating: I've been making my very own hot chocolate from scratch, every single day, since I was a kid! And", he cheered, "the whole spiel proves my real potential. After all, I can follow a recipe for an all-favorite old-fashioned top stove culinary art and perform a gastronomic delight. Gordon Ramsay will be so proud of me! Here, try it and have the courage to call your brother a liar!"

"Liar, liar, pants on fire!" shouted Onuțu an inch away from Vasile's nose. "What old-fashioned top stove culinary art? Boiling a kettle of water? Yeah, that's art to you! Dissolving a spoon of sugar and one of cocoa powder in a mug of hot water? Gastronomic delight a la Vasile! And you call it the secret for life longevity?!? Maybe, if you add a nanogram of arsenic or some alien chemical elements perhaps, not enough to kill you but enough to prolong a painful and miserable life! "

Vasile backed off. He stopped by the window. Down on the lawn, in the back of the house, two squirrels were chasing a white kitten. *The neighbor's cat must have given birth recently!* he thought, then he turned toward his brother, visibly annoyed:

"Why does every conversation with you necessarily lead to a fight? Why can't you see that Mom is trying to replace the old groceries with better products? After all, we don't need to survive out of the WIC program anymore" he said slowly. He circled the dining table, stopped behind his two- hundred- pound brother and, with steadily increased anger, spat out his guts: "Did you look in the mirror lately? You want sugar? Because that's all there is in that cereal you so crave: sugar! And the body does not know what to do with the enormous amounts of sugar you ingest every day, so it transforms into the fat that you see around your waist and your thighs and your butt. Does WalMart even carry underwear your size?". With that, he touched the sensitive spot he obviously aimed at.

Onuțu let the spoon fall in the bowl and splashed out the one ounce of milk left at the bottom. " I don't know how, but every talk around me stumbles into my weight! Everybody has at least one piece of advice for me on how to get rid of my belly or my butt! Not just you or Mom, but kids at school, in the gym, in church, on the street and the commercials on TV! This is all I hear: how to exercise, what foods to eat, pills and potions to buy and spells to enchant! I thought Mom said I inherited the genetic material from Grandma's siblings. They all looked like Rugby players. They were accepted the way they were, am I right? They had their lives, their food choices and their peace of mind when they sat at the table for a bowl of cereal. Why can't I?"

"And they all had short lives, they all had a fast death, of unknown conditions, including Grandma's father, your Great-grandpa" wisperred Vasile. "Did you know that he died when our mother's aunt was only two years old? He took a nap with her after lunch one day and he never woke up!"

Without taking in consideration his older brother's words, Onuțu continued his political-like sounding speech:

"Do you really want to know what we all need? Clean food! Basic nutrients! Vegetables from our garden, not from bordering countries! Fruits from our own trees, not mixt fruit in one hundred percent fruit juice coming from across oceans! Why can't we have a cow in the yard and fresh milk and cheese, chickens and eggs made two hours ago in our chicken coop? Why can't we bake our bread with wheat and corn cultivated in the United States? Find these answers and I'll lose weight! Everywhere you turn your head that's all there is: fast food, on sale processed food, affordable items coming from somewhere else, with God only knows what in them. I know where you come from! Believe me, I feel your embarrassment when I show up at your friends' gatherings! I'm just saying! You don't think I want to fit in and be accepted for who I am? Do you think I want to be fat? Do you think it is fun not to find something to fit in at Men's Wearhouse store? It's not! And I am very sorry, but I don't believe it is my fault! At least, not entirely! Our society set me up for failure! Where have I heard that? I don't recall, but it certainly sounds good! I love it! And you know what else? I am fine with a fast death at a young age!"

The atmosphere in the little kitchen/ dining room became really steamy. Gordon's scholars were boiling crab legs clearly not fast enough for their master!

Vasile, with his back toward his steamed up brother, was watching through the window the squirrels and the kitten still playing, now scrambling up the rocks behind the swing set. *Mom tried*, he thought. *She planted, year after year, a vegetable garden. Until she ultimately realized it was all a waste of time, energy and money. A lot more than what we ordinarily spend at City Market on fruits and vegetables. And, yes, mostly cultivated somewhere else, true, but,realistically, if you want to grow veggies up here, in the mountains, you need conditions!*

You need a greenhouse and irrigation. Otherwise, the hot summer days and the wind that never sleeps kill most of it. What's left, it's at creatures' mercy. Pack rats, chipmunks, squirrels, gophers, rabbits, with no sensitivity and no sense of value for one's hard work and effort, are all in for destruction, for murdering the helpless pricy plants and annoying the heck of the garden's owner. On purpose.

When he turned back to the kitchen table, his brother was just letting the last drop of expired almond milk down his throat, straight from the jug."Gone! No more milk! No more expired milk!" he muttered. A hilarious scene, one will say. Not Vasile. He said to himself: "You set yourself up for failure, bother!". And left the kitchen.

Chapter 2

Dynamite and Mozzarella cheese

Fake or not, the character of one individual who goes public will always make an impact on the public recipients. Nothing new. It happened in 1789, it is going to happen again in 2024!

Once the speech is out there in the wind, the representatives of mass media then divide the population in three well defined categories. The first category usually contains the affiliates, the ones who, even though are not awake yet and are not going to cut the hair into four ever, will follow that fellow to the end of time, never doubting him and never even asking themselves who paid off the dude's student loans. Because, by absurdity, if the new president will make everyone's student loan disappear, with an abracadabra bill, that matter will really not be of anyone's concern anyway!

Second category includes the opponents: those fellas will always be in disagreement with whatever the propaganda sells. They will find holes in the socks, even when the socks are still on Walmart's shelf, in an unopened package. They will reason with you about why you should not be eligible for loan forgiveness even though you do not own a student loan, you never attended a higher education program because you are just one of the millions of mediocres roaming around.

And, of course, last, but not the least, category number three: the indifferents. They do not share the beliefs of either the first or the second category representatives. They do not own any belief.

They live in their own space, usually limited to a room in their parents' house, have read all Stephen King's bestsellers, seen all Steven Spielberg's masterpieces, but will never ever raise their hand with a proposal or a vague idea of a change, an improvement to the process or anything that will help the society progress or thrive through a difficult time. They will not think that a leader should be replaced, no matter how many grandious grammar mistakes in a two- minute speech he makes. They will be the last ones to find out about Smith being fired over a fight with his supervisor, in the hallway, in front of lots of witnesses and regarding the lentils soup served at Thanksgiving. The soup, which was reheated a couple times, was spoiled. Who even cares? Nobody died!

"I found this on my son's computer desktop. It is supposed to be a five paragraph essay for English class. What do you, guys, think about? Good enough for a B+?" asked Bogdan looking for honest feedback from his audience. Nina was the first one with an opinion: " It's not a five paragraph essay! I counted three only: first category, second category and third category.

Three-paragraphs, I tell you. He needs two more!" she concluded and went back to file her rainbow double coated gel nails. Mihaela giggled in between two sips of her Venti Caramel Macchiato: "Clueless! You have no idea what a five paragraph essay means. Depending on the given subject, if you can arrange the sentences in a circle with five equal sectors, you are all set! Get rid of the word "fellas" and the B+ is guaranteed! Do you think we should start getting people up? It's after seven! The kitchen attendant will soon make waves. We should at least bring a couple of residents to the dining room to prove that we give a damn."

"You're probably right. We should not damage our frail relationship with the kitchen staff. If we need anything in this world to survive, that's food" philosophized Bogdan. "However, at the last all staff meeting, which you gracefully did not bless us with your presence, according to my humble recollection, we should always put residents rights first! In the light of that fact, if they want to sleep in and skip breakfast, shouldn't we grant their wish? And here is the moment when I feel my ego tickling and I compel to recite: After all, we are our residents' advocates!

Boy, how I envy those lawyers!"

A tiny old lady, gray hair and white sweater, passed by the nurses station. On her four-wheeled walker, she was carrying almost all that she had left: a beat-up purse overfilled with napkins, Hershey's milk chocolate Kisses candies and tissue papers, three pairs of pants and four matching tops, one pink fuzzy slipper and a week's worth of newspapers. She stopped and scrutinized the girls and the boy at the desk. Then, with an inquisitive tone of voice, she addressed them: "Where is my family? When are they coming to pick me up and take me home? They should be here by now!".

The tiny old lady with gray hair and white sweater revealed a hundred-of- times read letter: "They say I live here now. My daughters think this is the best place for me now because I am surrounded by nice people who can help me with all my needs. But I know what I need! I need to go back home! They can bring me groceries once in a while. I can still cook and keep a house."

Nina stood up. Softly, she grabbed the little old lady's arm and, protective and conspiratorial, guided her towards the dining room: "You are perfectly right! You do not need me at all. You will sit at the table, place the clothing protector over this beautiful white sweater and you are going to enjoy breakfast like never before. Yes, Marioara?"

"Yes", said the little old lady whose name was Marioara. "But I don't need the clothing protector!"

"How convenient!" said Cornelia, almost sobbing about the unbelievably happy ending of the story on the tiny screen. She stood up, closed the foldable tablet, stretched her whole body as far as she was able to and, in a ballerina manner, tiptoed out of the nurses station. "My episode is over. Let's get to work! People need to eat! Beds need to be made! Time is money! Is it pay day this coming Friday? Breakfast is the most important meal of the day! I'm going into the kitchen to sneak a couple of bacon strips. Anyone else wants some breakfast?"

"That's convenient?! What's so convenient? " asked Nina. "Not convenient for me, for sure! I will never pass the stupid skills test! Why do I need to memorize all those steps? Why can't I just go to the office, tell the lady in charge of the hiring process that I have given up all my dreams of becoming a model on Carrousel du Louvre and all I want right now is a nurse assistant position with the nursing home? Flat truth! No, sire! I need to watch a hundred times the YouTube video Skill number 10: Feed client who cannot feed himself and ask myself a hundred times why I need to clean the client's hands if the client is not even going to touch anything!?! I'm not going to pass! And this is my last straw, third time and I'm out! I can't do it, guys! I can't! I'm going back to waitressing! Against my will! Just to please those evaluators! They do think I'm dumb! Maybe I am dumb. Why do I sanitize someone's hands, if I am the one dealing with the fork, knife and cups?!? That's the question, Shakespeare!"

"Because, if your client has dementia, he will touch everything! Or, seeing that drumstick in the plate, he might want to grab it and hit you in the head with it! So, bottom line, his hands need to be squeaky clean as well as yours!" concluded Lizuca laughing from behind her desk in the back room of the nurses station.

Nurse Lizuca was wearing scrubs and nursing shoes for almost forty years. Not always the colorful tops she loves to switch today! Often she was recalling her first job, dressed in those tubular white gowns, buttoned in the back, with matching white shoes and cap, the ones you only find today in Halloween costumes alley. Many were wondering why was she still on the same payroll position? After all, she has the experience, she has the knowledge, all she has to do is apply for that managerial chair, jump through a few bureaucratic hoops (not to say bend over backwards!) and, voila! Her name will be on the door!

Well, let's see! She wasn't attracted to the leadership job from the get-go. Once upon a time, in her newbie nurse era, she witnessed, innocently, a hard-to-forget provincial conspiracy. Her boss was being attacked in a morning meeting with the plan of abolition from her function (read "kick out of her office") and total extirpation from the hospital's Pediatric ward, the same way a cancerous mole is excised. With her eyes closed and in total disbelief, Lizuca was listening to the "charges". She could still hear today the hissing sound hovering over the report room, that gloomy morning. All the nurses were present, some on their day off, going to the trouble of getting up so early in the morning to attend this macabre cabaret. One by one, they all pointed fingers and listed alphabetically the wrongdoings of the lady-boss during the years of her governance. The incident took place on the eleventh floor of the municipal hospital, right after the Revolution in her dear country. The general impression, at that very historical moment, was that, if you were a head of the department during the Communist Era, you needed to be eliminated. But the truth is, not all of those individuals were corrupted! Most of them didn't even care for politics! They cared for people! They did their jobs in the spirit of healing, of curing, of alleviating other people's physical and psychological issues. Young Lizuca knew the lady-boss very well because the lady-boss happened to be her practical instructor during the four long years of the nursing school. Her ears were still echoing her mentor's dreadful words: "Don't even bother! You did not immobilize his neck correctly. Inquire about a coffin and a spot in the cemetery. He is gone!" The nursing students shed hot tears on those lab manikins, but they learned, oh, boy, they've learnt! Lessons that stayed with Lizuca and helped her pass exam after exam, through job after job, in one continent after another continent, all her life! So, back to that anti-Communists debate morning, Lizuca felt an itch to the tip of her tongue and an invisible resort kicked her out of her seat. When all that anger was still clouding the brains, Lizuca, courteous and soft-spoken, reminded everyone of the wonderful deeds of the lady-boss, bringing in front of their blind-folded eyes the amazing woman and professional they wanted expelled. After her trembling but stunning ad-hoc presentation, the lady-boss remained in her position for many more years to come. She eventually left the hospital job, on her terms and for a totally different reason: to enjoy her grand-children. Secretly, Lizuca weighed that long-past intervention and was compensated by this sweet memory! And she never hungered to be in the shoes of her lady-boss. Wasn't in her stars, nor on her bucket list!

Today nurse Lizuca was happy, like any other day she is at work. Work is just part of her life and she values her life. She values everyone's life, around her and miles away. Every day is given to her as a gift, so she can use her abilities and her knowledge to craft something great. She finds existing happiness, laying here and there, everywhere, and she shapes it in different forms and sizes, adding smiles and hummed tunes, and then she shares it between those who happen to be around. That is her belief: You can't always change things the way you want them to be, but you can change the way you look at and feel about them. This principle guided her since twelve grade Psychology class. Along with one other: The more you give, the better chance to be reimbursed in Godly rewards, like the Bible says.

Nina, Cornelia, Mihaela and Bogdan are her sidekicks for the day, her helpers.

Bogdan is raising his children as a single parent. Lizuca, been there, done that, has all her admiration for him. She provokes him to talk about his children and the time he spends with them. She knows it will get easier, but never too easy. She praises him for being the father figure her own children never had. And she always remembered to reinforce the one advice she believes is dreadfully important: "Spend as much time as possible with your children; teach them your values and what you consider critical to know in life! Don't let the Youtubers raise your children! Learn from my mistakes!"

Bogdan was walking now from the end of the hall toward the dining room, arm in arm with a resident. The resident reminded Lizuca of the absent-minded professor character. Not because the movie was played and watched on the floor until the DVD succumbed, but because the resident looked indeed like Fred MacMurray. Or, at least, in her eyes did. They were passing by a trash can that suddenly grew wings. Not too strong though because it quickly crashed to the floor spreading its content on a three-foot radius circle. Couple of Red Bull empty cans rolled toward the nursing station.

Lizuca hurried and stopped one of them with the bottom of her shoe. "I am so disappointed!" she said softly. "I think I said a hundred times: We need to recycle! We can't just stuff everything in the trash! I know, behind my back, I am called the box lady, because I save every piece of cardboard I can to burn it and get it back in the ground as ash rather than let it be trashed on the landfield. I do the same thing with every piece of wood that I come across. Why to trash it? When it can be burnt and spread a little warmth before returning into the cycle of primary elements!" Glass, plastic, and paper need to be recycled!"

Cornelia whispered in Nina's ear: "She takes the dead flowers home, too, all the flower arrangements that should go in the trash, she takes them home and buries them on her land, up in the mountain. She thinks the flowers have souls and they must be treated like people. Crazy, ha?"

"Dynamite! Don't touch it! Dynamite!" the resident yelled while attempting to cover his head with the lower part of his hoodie. Bogdan threw himself on the floor and trapped the aluminum cans with the empty trash can right at the tip of Lizuca's foot.

"From the same meeting's powerpoints", he said victoriously. "Dementia care: the benefits of staying in their reality". He crawled all the way to the upside down plastic container, recovered the cans covertly hiding them in his pockets and jumped straight on his feet. "Skill completed!" he sneered toward Nina. "And I passed with flying colors, correct?"

After a second of panic, the young courtesy aide started to laugh a bit exaggeratedly , but definitely contagiously. "Flying, that's right!"

And almost no one paid attention when the resident got rid of his hoodie and, from behind the scratched bifocals, winked nonchalant and exclaimed:

"That was awesome!" And brought out of his pockets a handful of day (or two, or more) old Mozzarella sticks specifying "they are Dyno Nobel rolls!"

Chapter 3

Home

"I want to go home! Ma'am, I want to go home!"

At first, it sounded like the voice of a wounded soldier from a movie about world war two.

Close your eyes and imagine! In a foreign country, an improvised hospital room, on a bombarded street, with partially destroyed buildings, disciples of Florence Nightingale running from one Army cot to another Army cot, concerned not as much of the minutes required to scrub your hands during the handwashing process or seconds of frictioning your hands together when using hand sanitizer, but more about reinforcing blood-soaked bandages over limbs, torsos and heads of men dreaming to see again their porch in Ohio or Pennsylvania or California. Imagine those one-foot- in- the- burial- ground lads, in agony, not because the Oxycodone or Morphine Sulfate prescription was practically ignored by the pharmacy and received with delay, but because of the fear of never walking into their homes, never petting their dogs again! See them lying in their own body juices for uncounted hours, days at a time because they couldn't move and no one was around to move them or to elaborate a plan of care that states "repositioning every two hours will be provided".

"I want to go home! Ma'am?!? I want to go home!"

Now the voice reminds you of your four-year-old son left at the prekindergarten, in a dark corner of an old church room. He does not want to play with Lincoln logs or to color books or to make friends. All he wants is to be at home, in his modest room shared with his school-age siblings. It doesn't matter that they pick on him and make fun of him all the time. He looks at you with begging eyes and promises not to write again on the walls with permanent markers. Don't you feel like the worst mother or father ever? Don't you feel like you want to run away and never come back? You want to disappear to some other place where nobody knows you? You desire to lose the memory of ever having children? For a sparkle of a second, you wish all these could actually be possible, but, then, what will happen to your four-year-old son? Who will watch him grow up and go through all the childhood and adolescence stages, all the anxiety levels and the disappointments of not being the best athlete or not achieving the maximum grades, not being noticed by the one girl he really, really likes? You try to come up with scenarios where your four-year-old son will be taken in by a foster parents couple or a couple who cannot have kids for one reason or another. They will love him like their own, maybe they will be able to afford an in-home babysitter for the hours they must be away. They will homeschool him, teaching him whatever they consider necessary and in his own interest. They will discover his abilities, his natural gifts and talents encouraging him in one direction in which he will find success in life and fulfillment as a human being. What an utopian dream! What a fairytale!

So, will you really have the guts to leave and turn your back on your own flesh and blood?

After all, that four-year-old boy never asked to be born, never asked you to be part of your life. He never asked to come in this far- from- perfection world. Nobody asked him: "Hey, buddy, do you want to be my child?". You did not ask him: "Hey, dude, do you want to BE?". You just made him. You did not ask for his opinion either or not he agreed to be conceived.

And, plus, why will he be responsible for anything that is going on in your now-life? Divorce, constantly running between two full-time jobs, with two hours of sleep (because you heard Dr. Carter saying it is enough for recovering and you'll be able to take on another day), in the car, in the parking lot, with the phone by your ear so you'll hear the awful alarm, swish and spit Listerine in the flower bed and take on another eight-hour shift. And, after the whole naked sacrifice, an e-mail of insufficient funds in your bank account. Constant guilt that you can't bring home the other parent because you aren't good enough to have a life partner.

Oh, no! It's all on you, mate! Your child's happiness is really your problem. And you have to stay strong in your belief that everything you do for your child is the best you can do. Not the best that there is, but the best you can deliver. You have to put your trust in strangers you have never met before and believe they have the best intentions in regards to your child's education and upbringing. That education is going to slap you in the face one day, my friend! It's going to hit you like a boomerang! That day you are going to feel the urge to stand and speak against the toxic and controlling relationship your child is in, against the stressful job he or she has, against the misery you read in their eyes. Sadly, that won't be an option. Why? Because now it is their life, their choice, their acceptance. I do not kid you! I wish I was. Let me ask you this: how many grandparents in a hundred are happy about their children's accomplishments? Two out of a hundred? That's not even true. Almost all the grandmas and grandpas I know are complaining about the luck, (more like bad luck) of their off-springs. Those who are proud of their young family members have dementia. And you have to agree with them.

Nurse Lizuca confessed: "My grandmother used to say something like this: Those with children have to pray to God every day for energy and guidance in how to raise them right. Those who do not have children, they need to thank God every day and never ever ask God to give them children. I believe my grandmother was smart, although she raised seven children. She got even smarter after raising her grand-children! I never saw my grand-mother mad, not once in the twenty years I revolved around her orbit. She knew how to accept the things she couldn't change. She didn't have stomach ulcers either! But she had the guts to speak up her mind, that's for sure!"

Nina finished reciting the step-by-step one knee-high elastic stocking application and felt compelled to confess: "You know, as far as I remember, as a child, I always wanted to be the best. In everything: the best cheerleader, the one with the most choir solos, first chair in band for my instrument, straight "A"s in academics. I wanted to make my parents proud! In my mind, there wasn't greater joy than seeing my mother's tears of joy. My efforts in school were not for me, but for her. And look at me now: still struggling to find out what to do with my life. I still do not know what I am really good at and which path I should take on. Is it really nursing?!? Seems like way too many rules and regulations! A nurse does not abide by her own dedication to those in need. Above all, she has to care about state regulation, state surveyors, client's expectations, client's family expectations, pharmacy representative's allocution and the exhortations coming from other members of the team. Professional satisfaction practically does not exist; it is suffocated and extinguished by the anxiety and the fear of failing. Every day, no matter of shift, a nurse puts on not just her scrubs alone, but an invisible top layer iron shield, just to be prepared and be ready to face the avalanche of complaints coming from all directions, all levels and all sorts of individuals. From just these past eight weeks of hanging around here and a few venting frustration gossip sesions I overheard. Let's see! In one single shift, the nurse-in-charge was bombarded by:

Her supervisor: "You did not complete the risk management assessment on Mr. Popescu's last skin tear incident! Get to it ASAP!"

Her bath aide assistant: "Why didn't you tell Mrs. Popescu that I was busy (*scrolling to shopping links for dresses and shoes, perhaps!?*) and that's why I couldn't offer Mr. Popescu his scheduled bath?!"

Mrs. Popescu: "Yesterday, my husband got his supper late! It was cold and tasteless. I didn't even recognize what it was supposed to be! All mushy and floating in gravy. *(And they say there is no such thing as too much gravy!!)* I wouldn't taste it, not even for money! Also, he stinks! I don't think he was bathed at all this week!"

The occupational therapist: "I don't believe enough thickener is added to Mr. Popescu's prune juice. He is supposed to be on IDDSI Level 4: extremely thick consistency. Please, read the order and make sure his food is pureed and his fluids thickened accordingly, otherwise he's going to choke. His esophageal obstruction is pretty significant!"

The housekeeper: "It took me an hour to clean Mr. Popescu's room. On the wall, by the window, where he usually sits and eats sometimes, I found a gluey construction material-like, starting at the window seal and ending on the floor, on a little grayish clay puddle. I hardly got rid of it. No clue what it was: vomit or spilled food. It smelled like prunes!".

The kitchen manager: "It is not the responsibility of my kitchen attendant to thicken the liquids, just for the records! Nor is our fault that resident Popescu is always last to be served and, in consequence, his food is cold. The CNAs need to ask for the food and assist him with feeding in a timely manner. He is supposed to be supervised dining and I cannot help you there!".

Nina freezed for a moment with six of her fingers pointing out, searching her memory for more inculpatory facts, then she continued:

"If I was that nurse, with no time to use the restroom or running to the bathroom in the last moment, seconds before I wet my pants, I will stare at the pre or post menopausal face in the mirror and I will scold her, too: Don't you think it's your job to check with Mr. Popescu and make sure he answers a few questions? Just to clarify:

Do you want to eat pureed food and drink thickened fluids? Otherwise, why will you pour them down the walls? Be smart: spout them down the drain, in the bathroom sink!

Your wife feels you are not clean enough. Actually she was a bit more to the point and said that you stink! What do you think? Is today a good day for a bath in our brand new twelve thermal jets with hydro massage and effervescent bubbles? Or will you rather prefer a shower instead? Because these are the only choices I'm afraid you have. The hose off is out of the question!

By the way, are you happy with your life? Because I am anything but happy with mine!"

A soft buzz came from the phone in her pocket, but Nina ignored it; she was too eager to reach to the conclusion:

"You see what I mean? Do I really want to commit to this job for the next forty years?!? I must be insane to say "Yes" and I must be crazy to believe things will be different when or if I will be that nurse in charge".

Nurse Lizuca swallowed her saliva but refrained from commenting. The rookie's observations were pretty darn objective, she knew. Coming to America with the dream of being free to choose the life you want to have and her reality of the past twenty-some years were two very different things. It was sad and painful to accept the truth.

Nurse Lizuca remembered a quotation from Friedrich Nietzsche, hung on a friend's bathroom's wall, decades ago. She recited it softly and somewhat dramatically: "To live is to suffer, to survive is to find some meaning in the suffering". And, then, totally to herself: " I wonder if Friedrich Nietzsche knew someone like Mr. Popescu".

The man sitting in the farthest recliner of the common area tried again:

"Ma'am, I want to go home, Ma'am!" He was serious and grave. And he didn't think for one moment that his request was inappropriate. But, because no one was answering him, his patience got thin and he demanded: "Ma'am! Darn it! I have to go home!".

Mihaela approached him and addressed him with the most compassionate voice one is capable of:

"Mr. Popa, this is your home. You came here many, many years ago to spend the rest of your life. And, actually, I heard that you walked in on your two feet, with no front-wheels-walker, wheelchair or the idea of mechanical lift for transfers. You came with optimism and full of hope that you'll find here that dreamland place to rest your tired bones and muscles and the rest of your senses. You made this your home and we are here to take care of all your needs. Guess what? Today is your birthday!"

Enthusiastically, she gave him a big hug: "Happy, happy birthday, Mr. Popa! You are ninety-seven years young! Two of your daughters are arriving from Wisconsin, any moment now! They bring along a few grandkids, maybe even great-grand kids! They are all coming to visit you on your big day! That's why we need to try to keep this yellow shirt yellow, for selfies! I'm pretty sure they will bring that scrumptious chocolate cake that they bring every year! The one made from scratch following one of your wife's recipes, passed on from generation to generation! I know you like it so much! I also know that, afterwards, everything will look like chocolate!"

The man with soft white hair and the perfect yellow shirt started messing with the hearing aid from his right ear.

"I don't understand!" His voice sounded like a surrendering rebel. "Why can't I go home?" And continued with a bargaining attitude: "It's not that far! Couple blocks away, down by the railroad!"

Cornelia giggled: "He's probably talking about going home to Jesus! Two blocks from here, in the direction of the railroad, is the cemetery. He's probably tired of all the years lived in this home. 'Cause what's here to like? Push food, push fluids! Can't let them lose weight, God forbid! Invent new ways to fight dehydration! Popsicles! Five o'clock tea at three o'clock!

Rootbeer floats on the patio! Twenty-seven grams protein bars as supplements between meals! Who cares that they just finished a calorie overstuffed meal!

Then comes the nurse in charge:" Mr. Popa is on my list for no bowel movement in three days. Offer him prune juice, for Pete's sake! If there are no results by noon, I'll make him a Brown Cow."

Nina interrupted: "What's a Brown Cow?!?

Cornelia jumped up from her chair like a loose resort: "You never heard a nurse saying "I'm not going to jail because you haven't pooped! Here is a Brown Cow!?!? Then, sorry sister, you know absolutely nothing!"

With no invitation, she gushed out her knowledge: "Well, my dear apprentice, in nursing slang, a Brown Cow, sometimes, also called Black Cow, it's an original Macchiato invented by nurses in distress. Sort of a witches' brew, trust me! A hell-broth made out of prune juice, melted butter and Milk of Magnesia, warmed up in the microwave for ten seconds, just until butter bobless and shines at the top of the reserved cup. It's, also, a red flag for the CNAs on the floor. Either is working or not. Because, if the magic potion doesn't work, it means time for the magic bullet. And it's Show Time! Fireworks and poop explosions everywhere. The intervention is not recommended around Christmas, Thanksgiving, New Year or birthdays! You know why?

Because these are the most common situations when families are gathering around the tables to celebrate. Definitely not the eruption of a volcano full of shit, pardon my language! They come for selfies and to write complaints."

"Enough of that! I heard you loud and clear", said nurse Lizuca coming from the treatment room into the commons. "And you are wrong. They live here because their families can't provide the care they need in their home. Their spouses passed away and their children have their own lives, children, grandchildren and jobs, hobbies and responsibilities. Who are we to judge? God knows their situation, I don't! All I know is that we should be happy and we should feel good about being needed and being helpful. Now, please, change the batteries in Mr. Popa's hearing aids so he can hear Mihaela repeating herself on her adorable happy birthday, Mr. Popa! speech. Please!"

Nurse Lizuca walked to the glass door and looked outside into a backyard that was enclosed by an insurmountable iron fence. The trees were there for half of a century. They looked healthy, strong and were touching an angry sky with their dark green crowns. A heartless wind was working really hard on devastating a ravishing Shasta daisy rondel. Soon, large and heavy drops of cold rain started to knock on the glass door as ashy clouds hurried to hide the baby blue sky. The smell of the rain protruded through the walls squirming through memories.

Home. What is home? Where is home? Growing up in my parents house, in a room I was sharing with my brothers. That was home. Dreaming about getting married and having my own kitchen, I visualized my home smelling like peach cobbler coming out of the oven or strawberry and rhubarb jam simmering on the stove. Playing drums with the pots and pans and wooden spoons, three boys, Adam, Barbu and Călin, sitting on the floor and laughing their butts off. Fresh baked bread on the table and happy faces awaiting the food to be shared on the plates. Lilac bushes and sunflowers. Lace curtains in windows. Bedtime stories and snuggling before sleep will take us all into the dreamland. Porch where, on clear summer nights, will follow the Milky Way and the Big Dipper. Home is the last thing to disappear from the memory of a woman or a man suffering of Dementia.

Chapter 4

The letter

"Come here! Quickly! I want to show you something. Yesterday Tudor received a letter. Liana, the new activities coordinator, left it in his room , on the bedside table. I don't know if she's aware of how advanced his dementia is or was she planning to come back later to read it to him. But I was curious. Tudor doesn't receive a great deal of correspondence! Practically never. Okay, maybe at Christmas and on his birthday. So, after I got done with the two o'clock med pass, I took him in the gazebo and I read him the letter. Still feeling my hair standing up on my arms! It's that intense. That's why I want you to read it, too! I don't think he will mind. In fact, nevermind, he's in bed. I will just read it to him again. And you can listen. This way, can not be considered as a violation of privacy."

Magda was still young and still restless, still enthusiastic about her nursing carriere. Many years of experience in the nursing industry were resting on her shoulders, though she was never bragging about it. Never married, no kids, devoted and dedicated, heart and body, to her parents she was taking care of and her clients at work. Equally, perhaps, at times, getting more white hair during the hours spent in the nursing home then at home. She couldn't say she had lots of friends, but she was getting along well with the majority of people roaming around. Nurse Lizuca was her friend. Kind of. They both had the same ideas regarding recycling and they had similar views about culture, family values, life in general and claiming on the managerial ladder. They will forever remain common honeybees, working, not murmuring, no matter which hall or floor. God was their witness! When they were on duty during the same hours, the sun was gleaming warmth even on the most freezing days. Because of the few minutes they shared together.

The room seemed freshly painted but the smell of new was fading away. A light green color around locked windows and on the two parallel walls. A pleasant green. Not the meconium green and definitely not a Clostridium difficile colony green! More like the green of the snowdrops, Galanthus Amaryllidaceae, that bring their drooping bell-shaped flower out of the eternal snow even on stubborn winters with no intention of ever leaving. Nurse Lizuca remembered very well those tiny pretty flowers. She used to buy them on her way home from the High School classes. Small bunches, tied up with red and white twisted threads and offered for sale by Gypsy women, standing at the corner streets, between March first and eighth of March, the International Women's Day. It feels like an eternity ago!

Maybe the fresh paint smell was not there anymore mainly because of a devastating C. difficile infection that recently savaged the unit. That smell was still perceived.

Right about in the center of the square wall was a glittery speck left behind from a seasonal decoration. That little smudge was fully trapping Tudor's attention span. "Hello, Tudor!", buzzed in Magda. "Remember our visit we had yesterday and the letter from your sister you got and I read it to you? Well, nurse Lizuca here is intrigued too at the idea of a sister we had no clue you had and even more fascinated by the fact your sister sent you a letter so unexpectedly. I hope you don't mind if I read it again."

"Hello there, Tudor!", whispered nurse Lizuca. " Please, forgive our indiscretion and our unofficial barge in. It is pure curiosity, the kind of curiosity that killed the cat! Sorry!", apologized softly before squinting on the side of the Broda chair.

Tudor, with his eyes glued to the shiny speck on the wall, said absolutely nothing. Because Tudor said absolutely nothing for a number of years, since the stroke that left him forever stuck. He continued to stare at the foil tinsel garland crumb, in the center of the light green wall, like nothing was happening and nobody was around.

"Dear brother Tudorel!" started Magda trembling with emotion. "It's been a very long time since you and I have spoken. It's a shame! The same blood that flows in your veins, gurgles in mine too. Why do we accept this long nagging silence to cement between the two of us? I used to know everything about you: when did you last eat, what shirt I should iron for your meeting and how confident you were about an upcoming exam. Then, one day came and everything became suddenly invalid and like it never existed. You raised your voice at our mom pointing out that you don't appreciate the fact we were so poor. You put God and some other vulgar words in the same sentence, then stormed out the door and nobody knew anything about you for years. Like God was responsible for our financial situation! Wasn't His fault that our parents didn't know better and were not driven by ambition like you and I! Our parents lived by the slogan "We eat to live, not live to eat!" Pretty sure they never heard of Moliere's "The Miser", but we both remembered the fact there was no abundance in our pantry or in our refrigerator ever. Also, there was no sign showing that, somehow, those particular circumstances were ever going to change. Maybe that's why you left. Everything that we two had built together, as older sister and youngest brother, was gone. You were gone, out of sight maybe, but not out of my mind! It did hurt! Your silence did hurt! Not knowing under which bridge you were resting your darling curly hair and what garbage you were screening for food it was giving me nightmares and cold sweats! Then, one day, out of the blue, you sent mom those photos. You were handsome and were getting married! The clothes were expensive and the faces of those around you were content. We imagined your new life, new people, in a new place, with education that entitled you to a fancy job and a brand new house. Two little girls like two little angels and horses in the stables were completing the picture of a happy life. You didn't have to share! Still, I could own a tiny little room in a tiny little corner of your heart. You didn't think I deserved that! You were a changed person, a Tudor I haven't met before. You accused me of using our mother as a babysitter for my children. But you did not have the courage to look in my eyes and tell me, face-to-face, that mom can choose for herself where she wants to live and where to die. The sad side of this story is that mom did not die when she felt she was going to and, for almost a decade, she self-isolated from the entire world in her own home, like Napoleon on Saint Helena island. Everyone lost the Battle of Waterloo. Napoleon died, but mom still battles the loneliness and phantoms from the past. You put the distance between us and the silence grew thicker and colder separating us with cruelty. As if I had the cooties and you didn't want to be exposed. (Remember when you went to that summer camp and came home with a lousy present? That end of summer, lice turned our hair into their jungle gym, for sure. One hundred eggs a day and hatching up to nine days later! I got it out from Wikipedia, to be more convincing! We all got them. Still have the picture in front of my eyes: me with my head on the kitchen table and grandma, pulling the blood-sucking creature and their eggs from the scalp and each hosting hair in my head. Pediculosis capitis! Even pronouncing these two words makes me itchy! We did not have a chance! However, no one blamed you! We blamed the political regime!)

You could not stand the thought of having a sister! But I, even after being dumped out of your existence, I continued to be proud of you, telling everyone around me about my little brother and his accomplishments. Because you are and you'll be my little brother for the rest of my life, no matter how far your feelings push me away.

I decided to write to you now because I came to know about your unfortunate event, the stroke. And I am so sorry! Sorry for all the time we lost by being strangers by choice. Sorry for not letting our children enjoy each other as cousins. Sorry for trying to be at least as stubborn as you were and very sorry for not breaking the ice of the silence sooner. I understand that you need to live in a nursing home because of your needs. However, I'm planning to visit and assess the situation. It might be a possibility that will allow me to take you in my home! Wouldn't it be that nice?!? Especially now, that I am one of the seventy-six millions of empty nesters.

Can't wait to see you, hug you, kiss your bonny cheeks! With all my sisterly love,

Adriana-Gabriela"

Magda folded slowly and with broad respect the fine luxurious pinkish paper of Adriana-Gabriela's letter to Tudor. Her eyes were swimming in tears. Not the artificial tears that you buy over the counter, but real tears, produced by human compassion and nursing empathy. "Well, what do you think?" she forced herself to articulate in the end. But, before an answer could be born in that tiny universe, she looked at her simple leather band wrist watch and added breathlessly: "Hold that thought! I have to run upstairs! My pee-pee break was over eight minutes ago. They are most probably calling the cops to report a missing person: me. See you!" And disappeared fast from their sight.

Nurse Lizuca placed the letter between the pages of an old Bible on a shelf, cleaned a drooling discharge out of Tudor's imobile mouth and said really softly: "It was always a dilemma for me: do three-dimensional hearts have corners? And, with regards to your long-lost of sight sister, do you think you can find in your heart forgiveness in the same way she did forgive you? And, secondly, do you really think she could possibly take you into her home and care for you? Don't answer that! It's personal!"

Chapter 5

One way to become rich

"How many times did it cross your mind to make an appointment with a psychic, a palm-reader or a fortune-teller?" asked Onuțu working really hard to destroy a battalion of monsters in his video game. Vasile, busy with a homework project, lifted his eyes curiously:

"A fortune-teller? Hm! Probably never. Last time I had to acknowledge a fortune-teller, in fact a pretended fortune-teller, not even an authentic one, I was watching Disney's animated Robin Hood. Why do you ask? Did you happen to meet one? Did she tell you how to lose weight?"

Onuțu pretended not to hear the last comment: "Nah! I saw a TV advertisement. People are calling these psychics to find answers to their dilemmas, connections with their deceased loved ones or long-departed ancestors, advice for a stress-free life and, yes, how to deal with annoying brothers. I was wondering: can they lead you to the happy life of rich people? I mean can they see the way you can become filthy rich?"

Vasile stopped typing for a moment and meditated instead: "Okay, first: how many rich people do you know up close and personal and how do you know the fact that rich people are happy? Second: why will someone want you to be rich for just a dollar a minute? Don't you think if someone will be in possession of such info, he or she will use it for himself/ herself?"

"Not necessarily!" said Onuțu leaving the game, scooping his body out of the king size bean bag and grabbing an apple from the basket on the dining table. " They might see that specific something in your palm that you never thought of and just that small detail will give you the idea that will happen to be the key to your endless source of profit. Or notice something in the coffee grounds of your cup that will show you the money making strategy. Or a trip to the bottom of the ocean in search for the long lost treasure of Lima. One of my high school's teachers told us a creepy story once. Someone in their social club organized a tasseomancy session. They all drank Tazo tea, opened the bag and swiss-swashed it in the last cubic centimeter luke-warm liquid and turned the cups upside down. They invited a real expert in reading those patterns left by the tea leaves at the bottom of the cups. One of the participants was a woman having marital problems with an alcoholic husband. In the bottom of her cup a picture of the sinister hangman appeared and the message that was conveyed to her sounded like "Your problems will soon end". Unbelievably, her husband was driving intoxicated, had a car accident and died a few days later. Coincidence? Maybe. But scary, don't you think?!"

Biting with savor from the apple, Onuțu let himself fall back in the bean bag like an earthquake.

" Tasseography must have a satanic involvement, in my opinion" said Vasile grave. " And, once you fall in that direction, you automatically become a lost soul. However, I have to admit, I will struggle with the temptation of letting a palm-reader hold my hand and tell me where to start digging for gold. At least once. After that I'll be busy digging! He, he, he!"

"Well," started Onuțu with importance, "I did think of something original that might just make me rich. Just promise me you are not going to steal the pattern!" And, in great confidence, he exposed the make-me-rich plan to his all-ears brother. "Now and then, before I flush the toilet after a remarkable deposit, I cast a glance over the forms taken by my own fecal matter. Not kidding! I can see shapes of birds and animals, scenes of a whole live action, faces and expressions. Then, the very next moment, I make connections with my daily routine, my schedule for that day or the chance that I might be affected by an unforeseen cataclysmic failure. Let me exemplify: Last Monday, I visualized a shark with an open mouth full of devouring teeth. It was the day of the Math super test. Even though I considered myself well prepared, once I got that reading, I started to shake a bit inside. So, the first thing I did when I saw the Math teacher, was to ask her a few supplementary questions. The test went smoothly and predictably graced to my shark awareness !"

Vasile looked puzzled for a second, but the next second he realized what his brother was talking about and exclaimed: "A poop reading! The most ingenious idea of the century! What are you going to call it? Poop-ology?!? The art of reading fecal matter?!? Isn't this the stuff Cologuard does? But wait, how do you see making money with it?"

He joined his brother in the living room, sat on the carpet, in a Turkish position and, with nude curiosity, awaited the explanation. The explanation that came promptly:

"It will have to be a website where people will upload images of their own product. I will take a look at those uploads and, when I see something significant, I'll let the owner know. There will be a small fee involved, you know, to allow the photo entry. And, of course, there will be a method of payment, like Zelle, Venmo. Once the transaction is completed, I will communicate the report, strictly confidential. For instance: have patience, you'll inherit your uncle's estate. I saw a rainbow between his freshly dredged graveyard and a luxurious villa. Or: be extremely cautious today! Lucius Malfoy's face was all over the surface of your outcome!"

He took a deep breath, then continued:

"It is the same concept as in palm reading or tea leaves, coffee grounds or wine sediments patterns interpreting, but within the morphology of the byproduct in the toilet bowl. And the meaning of its configuration, in my personal, original, non-altered vision. After all, everything happens for a reason! The Universe trying to get in touch with your way of life is not new, but my vision of how to listen to it is genuine!"

Vasile tried very hard not to laugh and said:

"And when did you actually become aware of your gift, your talent? Was it when the wind took the cover of the hot tub and hit you in the head? Did you have a concussion and some never used section of your brain suddenly activated? Because, frankly, you know what I see? I see a GoToJail, GoDirectlyToJail, DoNotPassGo card. People are going to make you responsible for their actions based on your art of poop reading! You know, something like: "Yes, judge, I killed my uncle, but his death was going to happen anyway, it was in my poop database. Just a matter of time, I guess. He was going to die one way or another and me, being the only heir, I inherited the fortune, legally. Ask Onuțu if you don't believe me! He gave me the hint".

"Yah," said Onuțu deep in thought. "I might need a legal representative and props that will protect me from going to prison. However, in theory, it is doable. And the fact that nobody thought of this idea yet gives me goosebumps. Of course, after a while, I might be able to extend it to dogs and cats poop. How many dog and cat owners will do everything for the happiness of their pets!?! And think of the excitement of so many bored men and women ready to start a new, motivated and surprise-free life chapter. More greens my way! The veterinarians will start crocheting! I will put them out of business!"

Vasile was not listening any longer. With a sardonic laugh, he locked the bathroom door from inside promising his brother to become the number one customer of the newly self-proclaimed poop reader!

Chapter 6

One dozen of tamales

Cristina needed to raise money for her son's soccer team. She decided to make tamales and sell them at work. Everybody loves tamales! Not as much to make them, mostly to eat them. So Cristina called a few friends and together they made several dozens of chicken and pork and beef tamales. And chorizo. When all the work was done and the dishes and counters cleaned, they sat down, tired but happy, looking with satisfaction at the mountain of ziplock bags, each containing one dozen tamales, ready to be delivered to hungry mouths, not allergic to tamales.

"It will be interesting", said Cristina philosophically, "if somehow we could follow the tamales in the homes of those who will buy them and then just write the story, kind of a summary of their life. Then publish the collection under a title like 'The people that happened to help my fundraiser'. Will be rich in no time".

"Or they will sue you for not getting their permission to put their shit in the news. And they will be rich in no time", popped Cristina's husband's head through the door, but disappearing just as fast it appeared when Cristina threw a dirty towel in his direction.

"I can tell you a story right now", said Dana, one of the friends. "I am taking one bag to Marieta. She is home busy with her teenage son Ludovic. Did you guys hear what happened to him?"

Now Dana was capturing all their attention. Because none of them was aware of what happened to Ludovic. They heard about Marieta splitting from her husband Nelu a while ago. And because of that fact, Angelica, Marieta's youngest daughter, was refusing to attend school. But Ludovic? He was the best tenor sax in the High School's jazz band, also playing for fun in a small group that was meeting in someone's garage. Secretly, Ludovic was dreaming of becoming famous. Him and his beat-up saxophone. What could possibly happen to him?

"So, what is going on in that household?" asked Cristina with unveiled curiosity. And Dana started to unravel the story heard, first hand, from Marieta herself.

"Ludovic was sick, but he says he is sick whenever he doesn't feel like going to school. He pukes often or he has a hacking cough or, even better, diarrhea and vomiting, double dipping for an excuse. Marieta did not worry so much at first, but, when Ludovic did not get out of his room, two days in a row, she disobeyed the sign stating "Keep out! Man's cave. Enter at your own risk" and found her son boiling in his own sweat. Lying in bed, with some hundred and three degrees Fahrenheit body temperature. Pale like the high quality Irish butter, eyes sunken in their orbits, not seizing yet, but not answering her yellings either. She called 911, right away. They got to the hospital and, after some three-four hours waiting in the ER, the attending physician pronounced the verdict: ruptured appendix. And took Ludovic to OR".

Dana was proud of her "some hundred and three degrees Fahrenheit", like she was indeed the one who checked the boy's temperature, rectally, to be so precise. She was rolling her tongue with the ER and OR to make it sound even more serious than the emergency situation that Ludovic was caught in. She continued dead worried:

"Poor Marieta! It felt like the surgery lasted a day and a night! They had to clean each organ in the abdomen to make sure the kiddo was not going into septic shock".

Cristina smiled. Even though the event described was extremely serious and worrisome, she imagined each organ from Ludovic's abdominal cavity being taken out in a strainer and, one by one, jet off with a portable shower head, weighed and placed back in the abdominal cavity.

"By the time the surgeon came out to talk to Marieta, she was already thinking the worst. She had no more tears to cry, livid like a ghost, not eating or drinking for hours, she was so close to being an ER patient herself! Luckily, they got to go home that night".

"Wait, wait, wait! What?!?" interrupted Luminița another friend sitting at the table. "First of all, you said that Marieta did not eat or drink in hours. Are they not offering bottles of water and snacks to the family members nowadays? I remember a refrigerator with fresh fruit and beverages in the waiting room and a coffee, tea and hot cocoa machine."

"Nope, nowadays, with the budget cuts, they don't give you a free newspaper. And you need to bring your own flask with the drink of your choice. No restrictions!" winked Cristina, then added sadly: "But to go home, after such a dreadful operation, I haven't heard of!"

"Well," Dana recaptured everyone's attention, "here is the rest! The surgeon gave Marieta the on-the-spot education about the drain tubes he had to leave in place, like a map flags on Ludovic's abdomen, and how to change the abd pads when they get soiled. He explained that it will cost a fortune to have him admitted and hospitalized for the days of his recovery, so, it will be in everyone's best interest to just take him back to the clinic for follow up appointments at certain days intervals."

"That's impossible! I can't believe it!" shouted Raluca, another friend that helped with the tamales making. "You need to have your vital signs monitored for at least twenty-four hours! A complication might happen! He could die from an infection or an internal bleeding!"

"Thank God, he did not die!" continued Dana. "But, sure thing, Marieta has her hands full.

She had to buy her own wrist cuff blood pressure machine and oximeter. But that's really nothing. She has to stay home, on a leave of absence and watch him, day and night, like a hawk! That's why I

am getting these babies to her! They can all enjoy a nice, hot meal!".
And with that being said, she grabbed one of the ziplock bags from
the pile and sat a twenty dollar bill on the table. The first dozen of
tamales: sold and gone!

Chapter 7

What doesn't kill you, adds on to your emotional distress

"It won't kill you to go answer his light", attempted the young girl Cecilia to get out of the burden of responding to another call light. "Whatever happened between you two, it's in the past and should stay in the past. It happened so long ago that, surely, he already forgot about it! Most probably, it's just you, feeding an unnecessary sense of oppression which prevents you from shaking off the self-pitiness. That's all!" she concluded while scrolling the news headlights on her I-phone.

"You are right!", agreed Anica, a woman in between ages, hesitantly standing up from her seat. She, actually, was gobsmacked, shocked by the on-the-spot psychological assessment her decades-younger co-worker was able to pull off. But, instead of expressing the "Wow, you are good!" admiration, that will surely tickle Cecilia's ego, she decided to put on her big girl pants and show some good adulthood trends: "It is, probably, the right time for me to forgive and forget. And, like a good Christian I called myself, I will take the initiative. Another brick to my house in heaven can be counted today. Anyway, I am done with charting and I need to add extra steps for my cardio work".

Adopting an instant courageous attitude, Anica bounded all the way to the room. She stopped in front of the door from where the irritable buzzing calling sound was coming. She took a deep breath: *Leave the past in the past! Get over your grudge! It is time to let go! It's not worth it to stay upset forever. It gives you stomach ulcers and sleepless nights,* she thought and took another deep breath. *Why is it always so damn hard to admit our imperfection and step on our pride?!?*

"Knock, knock, it's Anica! What can I do for you, Mr.Ardelean?"

When her eyes met the eyes of the older man in the wheelchair and the musty odor of fungal infection drifted from the darkness of the compact room flooding her nares, Anica totally remembered the incident that took place a while back keeping her from caring at all for Mr. Ardelean for more than two years now. Here comes the story:

It was four thirty Ante Meridiem, after a painfully long night shift, with many miles on everyone's pedometer. Every morning, at half past four, Mr. Ardelean pushes his call button. It's time for his Sigvaris Compreflex calf wraps to be starting to fight Mr. Ardelean's chronic pedal edema. They are not really difficult to apply, it's more of a hassle dealing with Mr. Ardelean's strict routine of the stockings application or anything concerning his care, as a matter of fact.

Because, regardless of how hard you are trying to respect and be mindful of that routine, Mr. Ardelean will find a reason or two to teach you, one more time, "the right way", making you feel like an imbecile. Anica was not afraid of Mr. Ardelean; she knew how to redirect her feelings and, strategically, how to express her gratitude towards "the teacher". She's done it dozens of times proving herself stoic and meek. Sure enough, because of the longevity of the task, her shift will be over by the time she'll be done applying the socks. With a reinforced positive attitude, she entered Mr. Ardelean's room that morning, aforetime. She kneeled on the laminated wood flooring, with no problem. She poured a handful of unscented lotion (Mr.

Ardelean would not tolerate sissy stuff like lavender-scented lotion) and glided her gloved hands on the scaly skin of his weary limbs. "Make sure you stop before the toes" , echoed Mr. Ardelean's scratchy voice. "A blob of that matter will fire up a battery of fungus in between my toes and I will never get rid of it!" Anica has heard that remark a hundred times. It was almost amusing. Her nursing instructor, also, couldn't emphasize more to not use lotion between toes. She struggled to hide a smile that badly wanted to crack up. She bit her lower lip and followed with the compressive underliners. "Smoother them good, otherwise tonight I'll have Kielbasas for legs!" A funny scene from Disney's "Lady and the Tramp '', involving stolen sausages, flashed before her puffy eyelids. Still, she managed to suppress that smile and fastened in zig-zag the silky wraps. She was ready to stand up when the inevitable happened. Even though Mr. Ardelean's tone of voice changed into a sweet-tangy nuance, to Anica it sounded more like a heart attack: " You are already in the position, might as well do the blow job!" A devious short giggle was throning over the whole memory. Up to this day, it is not certain if it belonged to Anica or to Mr. Ardelean. What is for sure, Anica did not put on Mr. Ardelean's shoes that morning. With burning cheeks and uncried tears, she left his room humiliated and reluctant.

"Did she report the incident?" you might ask. She did, indeed. She caught the supervisor right before the change of shift report and, privately and indignantly, gave a skeletal description of the occurrence. A day later, she went into a detailed narration handed to the manager of the institution. She even filled out one of those orange grievance forms.

"And what was the consequence? What repercussions followed? " you may curiously want to know. Easy answer: nothing. Nothing was said. Nothing was done. But one thing: Anica was forbidden to enter Mr. Ardelean's room or to care for him again.

However, after all that water flowed down the river, she was ready to forgive and forget. So, knock-knock! Here she was, ready to help again, facing her fear of the unexpected. And she got it! From his wheelchair, in the corner of his fungus smelling room, Mr. Ardelean yelled in a hoarse voice: "Get out of here, you f—ing bitch!" Cristal-clear. Undoubtful and succulent.

"It didn't work!" Anica told Cecilia once she was back at the nursing station.

"What do you mean?" replied the young girl setting down her I-phone. "He didn't let you help him? Are you kidding me? Why not? What did he want anyway?" she asked and stormed away, to the rescue, disappointed and not at all curious for Anica's trembling explanation.

"I don't know. He asked me to get out of his room." Anica's voice was as flat as the Naan bread. On the outside, she seemed alright, her normal self, some will say, but, inside, she was running, covering miles of frozen snow, barefooted. *I wish I could turn in my resignation letter,* Anica thought and recalled a recent email she and her colleagues received. It sounded something like this:

"Respected Madames and Gentlemen!

My big day has arrived! Over the years, we watched our friends and co-workers reaching the Golden Age and retiring. Today is my turn to say Good-bye!

Several years ago (who counted them?)I opened the door of this facility looking for a job and an extended family. I found them both! I felt in the right place, at the right time and I embraced the idea "change is good". Holiday seasons came and passed, hot summers and stormy winters flew over our nest. My children grew up and found their own way in life. I had a good life here!

The people I cared for and the people I cared with became my own shield and comfort zone. I found strength and encouragement and I never felt alone. I have learnt every day, sometimes from mistakes, most of the time from exemplary people who, for a moment or longer, stopped by my side. I am thankful for them all!

Forgive me if I sound a bit emotional! Actually, I do experience new emotions. I don't have to go, but I know it is my time to do so. In my veins I have blood with nomad DNA. The time I spent here is the longest I have spent in any other place in my entire life. I believe that means something. It is important for me that you understand my point of view.

I also feel that there is something else, more or less related to nursing, that I want to try before my time is up. I would like the chance to discover what that might be.

With these being said, here is my two weeks' notice of intention to resign, though I really love to stay in a PRN position until the end of the month. This way I can exercise my right to use the Caring Angel parking spot. (Thank you, residents, for nominating, voting and presenting me this award! I am honored beyond words!)

I wish you all the best and I wish the best caring angels to come apply and work with you! Sincerely, yours!"

Anica felt soft shivers spasming her heart. Invisible both: to the naked eye and deaf ear. *Will I get there? To retirement time? I am not very optimistic about that! I might draw my last breath days before my actual retirement date. Because, what does not kill you right now, will, eventually, kill you slowly, but, definitely and ultimately, kill you. No doubt there!*

Chapter 8

A first day to remember, for what it's worth

Nurse Lizuca was giving orientation to the brand new nurse Domnica.

"Working in the so-called Memory unit (Why, in heaven, the word memory will be used to name a place with no memories, where the memory is a lost case? Bite me!) was an every day, no, every hour, every moment challenge. You never know what is going to happen next. "It's so quiet in here!" will dare to say someone from the front office making waves through the recliners occupied by sleepy and tired looking ninety years-old gentlemen. Ten seconds later hurricane Katrina will sink our world."

Domnica giggled: "You have a way of wording a crisis in development!". Lizuca continued:

"No, I am dead serious! You never say the word "quiet" inside of a nursing home! Never!

And especially inside of a unit where ninety-nine percent of its inhabitants suffer from dementia. The other one percent is represented by the chosen nurse, suffering from anxiety, sipping her seventh cup of coffee for the day, moving around like a prey or as if stepping on broken glass, if you please".

The two nurses stopped by the large window and watched black-capped Chickadees playing in colorful birdhouses made by the residents with the help of the activities department. Lizuca felt obliged to reinforce how important the subject was:

"Quiet is a forbidden word, a cursed word. The moment it sounds in a room full of Alzheimer's degenerated brains, the storm of the unknown and unpredictable could blast catastrophically in the very next given moment".

A gentleman, wearing a Polo sport attire by Ralph Lauren, stood up and, with the force of an iceberg in a guttural voice, yelled: "We are all gonna die!" Then, a perfect quiet zone. The silence settled in for exactly twenty-two seconds. Enough time to creep one up. The next thunderstruck hit the living room's ceiling with an even more catastrophizing prediction: "We are all gonna die!" The gentlemen did not move a muscle. He continued to stand holding onto the table motionless and rooted to the laminated flooring. His eyes were stuck on the opposite wall, where a painting of a superb mountain sunset with the silhouettes of two cowboys on horses was hung. Nurse Lizuca and nurse Domnica approached calmly and hardly hid their smiles.

"Indeed, we are, Mr. Radu, indeed we are" appeased Lizuca. "Every single one of us, at a certain time, on a sunny or a rainy day, at noon or the middle of the night, or in between, ready or not, happy or fed up, with peace of mind or swimming in a terrifying anxiety, bargaining with a deaf divinity or primed to get through the heaven's gates to sing with the angels, we are going to die one day. No doubt about it! However, I am telling you right now, Mr. Radu, it is not going to happen today! Not on my watch!"

The deck of cards Mr. Radu was shuffling for the past hour and half fanned out beneath the tables lined up in the living room. He stared at them through his bifocals but didn't make any sign of intention to retrieve them. A moment later, Mr. Popa, in his bright yellow shirt, holding a bowl full of chocolate cake mixed with cheesy scrambled eggs, filled a plastic spoon with the half-brown-half-yellow content and sling-shot it precisely to the Apocalypse predicting Mr. Radu's spectacles. Bulls eye! The mixed-up plat du jour sample slided nonchalantly, from the surface of the glasses, alongside the front of Mr. Radu's Polo shirt. Nobody laughed, but a creepy screechy impression from underneath a Broncos blanket covering a slim silhouette curled up on a close by couch made the hair on the arms of the two nurses stand.

And this is the moment when Mr. Barbulescu walked toward the kitchenette, grabbed the handset of the telephone on the wall jack and, before the nurses realized his intention, he dialed the three basic numbers and was on the phone carrying this conversation with the 9-1-1 operator: "I'm held hostage in this dump! A food fight and a pillows fight are going on simultaneously. Parakeets and hummingbirds feathers drift over the chocolate cake and nobody gives a damn! My wife and I used to own the building and rent it out to undocumented refugees, but now that the government took over, the Nazis are out of control. Send in the cops!"

The cops did show up and the social worker did have to leave her food on the plate, on her birthday, to rush on scene, to implement the fifteen minute checks on all involved parties.

"You had the chance to experience the chaos in full effect" concluded nurse Lizuca. "Sometimes, this will happen at two after midnight and, believe me, no one will be happy for a prank like this. Unfortunately, here it is not considered bluff, an investigation has to take place, a report has to be made and fifteen minute checks on half of the population in the Memory unit, will be strictly documented for a whole week, or month or year, depending on the gravity of the facts and the side of the bed the social worker got up."

Nurse Lizuca commenced to show Domnica the incident form and other necessary documentation needed to be done, when, suddenly, she remembered:

"While the commotion was resurrecting the whole dining room and we were busy calming down the spirits, across the hall, locked in the bathroom, Mr. Apetrii was totally enjoying a wall finger painting using the cheapest product on Earth and today's market: freshly delivered, formed consistency, own feces. (*Too bad photos are not allowed to be taken here! Onuțu will be thrilled at reading these blueprints!)* At the expense of poor Mihaela, stuck there for an hour cleaning poop from everywhere. She will call in sick tomorrow, more likely, sick of it."

"I don't know if I will show up tomorrow either," murmured Domnica pale. "The welcome I got today was rather discouraging than warm and full of hope. I left the OR for a less animated workplace."

She was about to say "quite job", but remembered, just in time, the word "quite" was prohibited.

The ring of the phone, on the desk by the computer screen, startled both of the nurses focusing on charting. Lizuca answered promptly. She stated the super long name of the facility, followed by her name and credentials.

I will never memorize this professional greeting, thought Domnica.

"It's for you!" said Lizuca, handing the phone to Domnica. The color of the cheeks in the new nurse's face disappeared completely after the person at the other end conveyed the news: her twelve years old son Andrei was seriously injured and she was expected to pick him up ASAP. She apologized to Lizuca, swiped her badge by the sensor of the door to the secure unit and, after a pit stop in the manager's office, left at once.

At about the same time, the nurse from the other hall on the first floor stormed in and put the keys from the medication cart in Lizuca's hand. Her ash-colored face was a prognostic for catastrophe. Her trembling hands were clammy and she barely could articulate a few strangulated words: "My daughter overdosed. The ER called. I must go!"

Lizuca stayed behind, like paralyzed, mute and terrified. She thought of black cats crossing in front of her car, empty water buckets, full moons with halos and spiders falling from the ceiling. She remembered her dream about the pila of snakes in the toilet bowl. But nothing compared to the dreadful fear of losing a child.

The rainy storm started with no warning. Angry drops of water were hitting the metal roof with the sound of hopelessness. Lizuca opened the patio door and let the cold natural gobbets hit her burning face. Natural tears and nature's trickles merged and mingled in an amalgam of feelings. An amplified thunder and lightning happened right there in the backyard and forced the nurse back to her duties.

Chapter 9

Kiss football Good-bye, babe!

There hasn't been one day (or night) without dreaming of becoming a football player!

Especially since his body started to show attributes of a footballer. He was almost as tall as his four years older brother, he had strong leg muscles and, even though the physical education was not super attractive to, he had daydreams of wearing the custom football uniform. Because his mother was helping the Rec Center coaching soccer, Andrei had to play soccer, just like his brother, since kindergarten.

One day, in the mail, his mother received a letter of invitation from the local football club. He was invited to join his city's football team! It was his chance and he was not going to lose it!

After several discussions, promises to help with chores and not to get concussions, he was on his way to step on Peyton Manning's large footprints.

It wasn't free. It wasn't cheap! But he promised to keep his grades up and his mother signed the enrolment form and the check. She made it very clear that it was against her gut feeling, but she wanted him to be happy, to follow his dream.

The practices were different compared to soccer. There were technique training, tactics exercises, speed drills, defense and offense skills to be learned. Not easy and not always painless. Hidden tears and swallowed pride! *I want to do this! I want to be good at this!* thought Andrei one hundred and one times.

And here it was: the day of the last practice before the first game! Not entirely sure he was ready to face the adversary, but he was familiar with lots of strategic game plans. The greatest fear had to do with teamwork. His teammates were not always supportive of each other. *Your teammates don't care how much you know until they know how much you care* did not make a lot of sense just yet. And there was a lot of criticism. Mistakes were pointed out with no mercy and plenty of sarcasm. Seemed like everyone was breathing football, but him.

"Go back to your country!" whispers were not isolated incidents. *What do you mean by going back to my country? I was born here! This is my country! I have the American flag flown outside my home with pride and my father served in the US Army for many years. This is my country!*

Are you bothered by my mom's foreign accent? So what if she was born somewhere else? She is now a naturalized American citizen. She knows American history and her grammar is impeccable! Your attitude is despicable! Andrei wished he could scream his thoughts out, loud and clear. But he couldn't. He knew better! He was taught to be polite and considerate of other people's feelings. He did not think like those teammates and did not share similar feelings. On the other hand, he could not share these feelings with his mother either because he was afraid she would get her feelings hurt! Talking to the coaches about this issue? No way! This wasn't preschool or kindergarten! They were teenage boys very much aware of bullying consequences and racial segregation true meaning! Plus, you don't believe the coaches were suffering from a common form/ bad case of selective hearing?!? They know what is going on. They just don't know how to handle it.

Domnica arrived at the school's gridiron. Her head was spinning. Anxiety was tightening her six hundred muscles in her body. Strands of all sorts of speculated scenarios were mulling over a scrutinized brain. *I need him to be okay! If only nothing major happened!* She spotted the group of people hunchbacked or sitting on the field all the way to the furthest side. She started to run faster and faster. Her son was lying down. His dirty blond long hair was wet. His eyes were swimming in uncried tears. He saw his poor mother approaching and started to murmur softly at first, but louder and clearer by the time she arrived at his site. "I'm so sorry! Mom, I'm so sorry! My leg is broken". The mother's facial tension dissipated almost instantly. A broken leg, phew! Easy fix! The coaches carried Andrei to the car. No one said anything until the boy was sat in the back seat. Only then one of them announced: "You will be refunded. You will get your money back. It will be a check sent to you by mail. Return the uniform and helmet when you can. Wait, I think the helmet must still be on the field, don't worry about it!"

Domnica started the car. In just a few minutes they will be at the hospital, for the x-rays and an operative or non-surgical fixation. Maybe just a cast or removable brace. She was breathing regularly and her heart rate was settling.

Andrei was reliving the moments right before the accident. He experienced again the glorifying feeling of getting the ball and running like helped by invisible wings. A black hole in the memory, then the pain invading from all directions. A teammate sitting on his leg hissing between his carious teeth: "Kiss football Good-by, babe!"

Chapter 10

Too much poop in the world

"Do you have any parfum with you?" asked Mihaela secretly in the ear of her partner for the shift, Tatiana. "Yesterday I had to clean the walls in Mr. Apetrii's bathroom, the sink, mirror, his bottom and underneath his nails. I don't really know if he got a Brown Cow prior to that, but surely he had an X, X, Xtra large bowel movement! I had no clue how to chart it in the matter of size, so I put down two large formed BMs. If I close my eyes, I still have the motion picture of the time I spent in that horrific smell! I imagine this must be the atmosphere in the Morgue or around bodies in some degree of decomposition. It was like someone had died there last month and I was the lucky one to discover it. The smell is still fresh in my brain! I'm not kidding you!"

Tatiana, too, young and fairly new in the line of work, was searching inside a huge backpack, unable to hide her genuinely spontaneous smile. Not that she wasn't feeling for her co-worker, she did, but she had a wild imagination and the scene presented was too hilarious not to be amused. With the eyes of her mind, she could see Mihaela scraping the poopy surfaces with a nail file. *O,o,o nobody said anything about a nail file! Don't go too far!*

"Finally", Tatiana exclaimed, getting her head out from the rucksack which seems to contain everything else but her kitchen sink! "I have exactly what you need!" And handed Mihaela a small round metal box with the letters Y and R visible on the lid. "It's French. Solid perfume.

Plein Soleil by Yves Rocher. Hope you like it! I love it!"

Mihaela took one pink glove out of her pocket, managed to break it by putting it on her right hand. "Damn it! Made in China piece of shit!" muttered visibly annoyed. With her right index, still covered by part of the pinkish synthetic rubber, moved smoothly over the round tin's content.

Once she thought enough creamy butter remained on the glove, she pushed her finger as far as she could into her nostrils and tried, with circular fast motions, to leave the scented cream to the olfactory sense. "Mmm!" she sobbed. "This is the exact antidote I was hoping for! I am really stressed! A complete wreck. Plus, I didn't sleep enough last night. It took me a long time to conceive an Incident witness statement the director asked me to. Listen to it!

"It happened soon after midnight. Nurse Lizuca was calibrating the glucometers. My partner Ramona answered Mr. Ardeleanu's call light. He was wanting something for itching. I accompanied nurse Lizuca to his room and watched her applying Lychadrin lotion over his itchy spots. This is when Ramona came in the room in a hurry and asked us to follow her fast. I knew it was an emergency, not a joke.

We found Mr. Popa on the floor, in his bathroom. I close my eyes and see that picture on and on! Mr. Popa's body was crushed in between the toilet and the sink, with his head underneath the sink. Both eyes opened. Fixed and not reactive to light. His skin was pale and still warm to touch. I touched him. I tried to pull up his trousers and the underwear found down to his ankles. We all kneeled down and, very gently, pulled Mr. Popa's body toward the center of the bathroom's floor. Nurse Lizuca kept on repeating herself *I can't find his pulse*, checking both places: peripheral and at the carotid. He did not respond to any of the external stimuli we tried. Nurse Lizuca ran to the nurses station to check on his DNR status. He was a Full Code. At this time, nurse Lizuca called upstairs asking nurse Emilia to call 9-1-1 and to send us more help.

When she came back she brought the crash cart with her. We rolled Mr. Popa onto the wooden board (What were we thinking?!?

He was already on a hard surface!) and started CPR. Nurse Lizuca used the manual resuscitator with mask and flow diverter. Ramona and myself took turns at chest compressions. We had to remove Mr. Popa's dentures; they were stuck to his gums (too much Fixodent!). Other observations: Mr. Popa had shoes on, on the bathroom floor we did not observe any urine, feces, vomitus or other fluids (like water). No signs of trauma (skin tears, bruises) and no blood could be seen.

Paramedics arrived and pronounced his death at 0050. They were saying something like A-fib. We were unable to move the body from the bathroom and we had to leave it on the floor because it was considered a "coroner's case".

I heard nurse Lizuca talking on the phone with Mr. Popa's POA or next of kin, I am not sure who it was.

The coroner came together with the Funeral Home representative. They conducted a short investigation and concluded it was no foul play, perhaps a massive heart attack or stroke.

That's all I witnessed."

"And my signature at the bottom. What do you think? Is it too personal? Did I get tangled in too many details? Is it bad I used names? Can I have a little more of that plain sun smelly thingy? What is it called?"

The answers never came. Nina stormed into the back room of the nursing station, short of breath and puffed out the bad news:

" The new resident in room 101 is out of bed!" "And?" Both Tatiana and Mihaela exclaimed.

"And he took off his trousers, pooped on the floor a couple of summer sausage's size, fat BMs (*Onuțu are you getting this picture?!/)* and stepped once or twice in them. It's everywhere! And that's not all. The pretty lady in room 121, Florica, is helping him clean up! It is hilarious!"

Tatiana opened the Yves Rocher tin again, shared with her friends and applied some of the solid perfume in her own nose and said:

"Let's do it! The one thing nobody talks to you during the hiring process is how many hundreds of pounds of crap, cramped in hundreds of yellow barrels, you are going to handle in a two week period, for that trifling, meager and trivial paycheck, that will never be enough! It's like today is payday and tomorrow you are broke again".

Leaving the nurses station, Tatiana remembered:

"It's still a secret, but soon everyone will find out: nurse Magda is quitting. She was under some sort of investigation. I guess one family member made a formal complaint against her. Supposedly, nurse Magda took her sweet time applying a cream to a female resident's buttock over a superficial pressure sore. The female resident made a joke over breakfast with family about nurse Magda, something like "the nurse enjoyed herself doctoring my butt", but the family member considered the incident inappropriate and contacted the administrator. The administrator investigated nurse Magda's sexual orientation and other hobbies, over the phone, during a forty-five minute questionnaire that, he said, was mandatory. Nurse Magda swore not to put up with the circus any longer and, the next day, turned in her resignation. What a loss!"

One of the dirtiest jobs on planet Earth took place in room 101. It was now completed. The girls were back at the sink, effectively washing their hands, following the step-by-step bilingual laminated poster EcoLab 92632047 on Amazon, on the wall, at the tip of their noses.

"What a shitty day! And it just started! Hey, did you know?! Somebody left tamales in the breakroom refrigerator. Let's warm them up in the microwave and have some with my new hot sauce See Dick Burn!" invited Tatiana with a mysterious smile cracking up. "My brothers were fooled by the innocent label with the blue sky, happy sun and the caricaturistic dick on fire.

Perhaps it was a bit too much ghost pepper mash added to the green chili we were having! I watched them slowly transforming into fire-breathing dragons! I laughed copiously."

"Were you not affected at all by the deadly sauce? Or maybe your taste buds were affected by the Covid infection you recently had and you can't taste anything!" Mihaela threw her assumption in the air.

Tatiana was waiting for that: "Nope, my taste sense is intact and better than ever. However, the hot sauce can't harm me because … I don't have a dick!"

"But you have balls, girl!" concluded Mihaela.

The girls rushed towards the tamales while a resident in a wheelchair, happening to be nearby and happening to be listening to their conversation, exclaimed:

"CRAZY!"

Chapter 11

In A Perfect World

Cristina glanced one last time at the newly created Word document. Closed the device and placed it in the "Coffee, Scrubs and Rubber Gloves" everyday go- to- work bag. *I should pack the cord also. Just in case the battery is low. I don't believe I am capable of a from-the-heart-by-heart speech. I need to peek. I don't want to make a fool out of myself. All my friends will attend. I should look professional!*

The email inviting everyone to the All Staff monthly meeting was very clear: *Please, bring any comments, any suggestions, anything you believe will improve our communication and work atmosphere in general. We need your input!* And was signed: *The Management.* Based on that incentivized call, Cristina wrote the following short presentation:

"I am a nurse assistant, a CNA. I strive to treat everyone the way everyone treats me. Oh, no! Correction: The same way I wish everyone would treat me! I made the correction because I feel I am not always treated with the respect and the consideration I deserve. My work, our work is not forget-me-not by ear desk job. It requires a lot of energy. I run all day. On a good day, eight thousand steps on the pedometer. On a not-too-good day, it could go up to twelve thousand steps recorded by the monitor. And that's not all I do, running. Beside that, I do the work, the tasks, the assignments, the chores. Taking care of others is not easy stuff. It requires responsibility, knowledge, accountability and muscles. Sometimes I answer a call all the way at the end of the longest hall in the building to find out that the light did turn on itself. "I didn't touch it! I don't know what happened! But now that you are here, please move the water pitcher a few inches. It bothers me. I can't see the television entirely." In a perfect world, all the rooms will be lined up in a circle, right there at my fingertips (toe tips). And the water pitchers will be placed on the bedside tables, within resident's reach,never blocking the TV's visual field.

Other times, I answer a call for help with personal care and I am not able to locate the wipes, or the disposable undergarments, or the moisturizing lotion and I must make the special trip for supplies in order to do the job. In a perfect world, the closets will always be stocked and all the products will be available, right there, at my discretion.

Sometimes I come to work and, surprise, I am to go to a different neighborhood that I expect or the on-line schedule says. That irritates the heck out of me and throws off the good intention and positive attitude I had when I clocked-in. In a perfect world, I will be able to keep my emotions in check-mate, never give room to angry outbursts and never, ever blame others for my irascibility.

When I open the work email, an avalanche of demands are striking my brain cells. No matter how much I do or how proficient I try to maintain myself, it is never enough and never good enough for nobody. My partners are crying out, the families are complaining, the residents are not happy, the other departments feel frustrated. New tricks are to be learnt, acknowledged and receipt of acknowledgement sent to the appropriate party. Demands, demands and more demands. When, in the perfect world, the emails in the inbox and the outgoing ones will contain flowers, butterflies and rhymes, you know, like *Roses are red/ Violets are blue/ I know you need me/ I'll tolerate you.* Because, actually, Earth's skies are violet, we just see them as blue. I don't really know why I said that here. Maybe because it rhymes! Oh, and lots and lots of happy faces with tears of joy.

Often, I have to click links and watch educational lectures on how to do my job. But, you know what? The nurses under whose licenses we work, don't live in the perfect world either. They receive emails with attachments or URLs links to Youtube videos on how to place a vaginal Estring. That's evolution! Female residents do not need to make the trip to specialized health providers! Your good old in-house practical nurses, Autodidacticism followers, geniuses and Youtube graduates will do the five hundreds dollars job for less than seven dollars and fifty cents. You can't get better than that!

After a twelve hour shift, I clock out and run home trying to be a loving mother and wife. In a perfect world, dinner will be on the table and food will be not too hot and not too cold, but just right.

I apologize! Did I offend somebody? I am sorry! Wait! I do have a positive remark to make. The other day, a group of friends of mine made tamales for the school fundraiser. We cooked with love, packed them in dozens and sold them right away. One thing we did not do: we did not taste them. We trusted our judgment and prayed for the best tamales ever. My daughter is enrolled in the CNA class at the college and had a day of clinical experience at the hospital.

She shared with me impressions from this experience. She mentioned cases of drug overdose and fractures and other medical problems. But she also told me that in one of the break rooms at the hospital there were tamales in the refrigerator and a note on the table: *Please, enjoy tamales made by wonderful people, for awesome people! And thank you for taking care of my child today!* There were more tamales than needed, so my daughter had one and brought me one at the end of the day. It was one of our tamales!

Conclusion: We might not live in a perfect world but our world is truly amazing! Thank you."

Cristina arrived at the meeting just in time. She signed the attendance form and heard the administrator's opening statement. "We have guests from the governing board. The Board of Directors representatives brought their own agenda. Please welcome them and be open to their suggested programs. Thank you to all of you who came prepared with the input material I asked for. We will accommodate that at a later time."

It is not the end!